TEENAGER LIFE CHAPTER-LOVE

TEENAGER LOVE.

LAKSHYA SARAFF

This is presented as a work of fiction and dedicated to nobody.

(Nobody is perfect,

My crush is perfect,

So my crush is "nobody".)

Contents

Acknowledgements

Writing is one of the most easy-looking jobs. But indeed it is one of the most difficult jobs one can take up. It is more difficult and rewarding than a human mind can interpret. I would like to thank each and everyone in this book to be a constant means of motivation in my life. For never leaving when I was alone. And, I hope someday we meet just because of one of these books. Never leaving my side during my lows and celebrating along in my highs. You have shown me what real friendship looks like.

My journey on the campus because of whose existence this book is possible is a journey in progress. But looking back at the time when I first entered the campus, I might have never thought to be writing a book about my crushes and girlfriends.

Preface

Before I get to the book I would really like to point out that a girl who's your friend is your girlfriend and likewise for guys. So, please stop calling your dates as your girl/boy friends.

This book is open to anybody my age, not just me. Because all the teenagers go around the same question.

What really is love?

It's a strange question because most readers associate love with happiness. But is this the case? Is it something you feel you have for someone? When you claim she's my crush, do you truly mean it, or is it merely an obsession that arose as a result of a modest gesture by the other person You can only love someone if you know about them, if you know their darkest secrets, and you only know that if you are friends with them. So the issue now is, "Is friendship, love?" It is, indeed.

Is friendship compatible with love?

It is, indeed. A friend is similar to a parent to a teenager. In my opinion, a buddy is typically sought by the other sex because a guy is always insecure about himself, and a girl is too, but in a different way. As a result, a recommendation from the other sex is a true godsend.

But, in the end, we end up with two different answers. One from the mind, and the other from the heart. The mind might say that it's just an attraction, but the heart is a soft spot in a guy. And we fall for the small gestures towards us. That's what happened to me. So, this is my story.

See you in the end, until then sit back and enjoy the roller coaster of a ride of my love life.

Prologue

The people in this book are those I have been close to in my so ongoing journey in G.D.G.P.S. Some of them have left this small world we had in between the walls of the campus. Yet they will always be in my heart. Mom- Dad, I hope you never find this book but if you do, don't think a lot before giving me a pat on my back. After all, I am a teenager with a pen trying to voice out the deep feelings of a teen in love.

When you think that we're just children with no sense of love, please just think about it when we love you back, that is love and when it is shown to someone else it's not love.

What you're going to do is dive into is a very small piece of the feelings of a teenager. With all that mood swings daily. A female goes through mood swings during periods, but a teenager goes through it every single day. And a teenage girl doubles it during her periods.

CHAPTER ONE

Love....

Love is not just a word. It is poetry in itself. How do you know you're in love? You don't have to know about it, your heart tells it to you when you don't understand the sleepless nights just thinking about the same person. The lost mind and soul... The feeling of loneliness when they are not around. The journey from wanting presents from people to the presence of ONE person. That is love. Love is not just wanting a person for yourself. You'd want them to be with you in your memories and all the ups and downs. You want them to be with you on their cute and sweet terms. Them to be protective towards you. They accept you as their best friend, share their problems, and talk to you as if you are their diary. Love is when you are hurt all the time. Nothing seems alright, but you still want the same person to love you back over and over again. You know the fact that starting a relationship is very easy, ending it is nowhere behind it's easier. But the fight you have to fight every single moment for your love is the hardest part of any relationship. And that my friends are where we lack, we all lack commitment to love. I might sound fanatic when I say that one must date their best friend only because your best friend is the only person who will know you the best. They know when you are sad, when you need to be cheered or when you need some space. Everyone in this world has this one person who is equally retarded as themselves.

Love is that moment when you want to cry with the other person, but you can't because you won't cry if the two of you are together because there won't be any sadness in your life after you. You might never know when the other person is faking around you, but the fact is that you have your brother here telling you about it. A person who truly loves you might never buy you costly gifts, but whatever he can, he'll gift it to you with all the love and respect he has in his heart. He might not be able to defend you always but he will stand up for you even if he knows that could mean the end of him. He will care for you more than himself and sometimes even tell you, but that does not mean he is doing a favor that just means he's had a bad day and needs you with him. He will always be there for you even if it is at 3 at night. (Well, if you call me at 3 AM, I'll kill you please remember that). He will be jealous if you talk to others, but never shows it. For him, you might be the most important person on earth. Even if he has very less time with someone else, he would prefer being with you instead of that person. That's love. He doesn't want anything from you in return, he wants one simple thing that too is not because he is doing so much for you, but that's because he is a human and has a heart, he expects you to stay with him forever and never leave his side. True love can't be expressed in the words "I love you" or "you are my life" but it is expressed with all the moments you cherish together. All the moments if they are memorable. When you read the chats, you just smile and you are lost in that moment. You want to be there and you just wish you could have said so much more, but you, can't you then think of telling them now, but you can't because true love is expressed by the time the other person unblocks you after a fight.

There are 3 things that people mistake being one amongst all of them. People usually misinterpret flirting or lust as love. But is it? flirting is just loving someone's words to me, whereas lust is when you fall for someone's beauty but LOVE...... When you fall for the soul everything about the other person the way they present themselves in the way they treat people when you fall for the other person you will want nothing just their silent presence will give you peace.

You will know it's that when you go around meet different people, and visit different places, but the void deep in your heart still exists longing for someone. Someone you did not be with, in the place of these trips.

It is that sensation when you are among all the people in the crowd you are glad that one particular person was there with you.

Love can't exist without fear. If the fear of losing the other person doesn't scare the shit out of you, my friend you were never in love.

CHAPTER TWO

First Attraction...

I have had a few so-called "crushes" in my life, it remained for a day or two (infatuations) then poof!! I won't call all of them "crushes" cuz a crush is one-sided love but I just liked them. You like your friends, you just don't like them you love them. But friendship is also love with you impart when you want to, it's unconditional for me, although some people have the varying one.

Wait, I almost missed it. Let me Introduce myself. Hi everyone I am one of you, a human with feelings. Other humans call me with a name which goes like "Lakshya". I am when this book was written a class 11 student. So, where was I..

.

I found the real meaning of the word "love" or "crush" in 6th grade. Many take time to find a perfect girl, but I had found one then. She's one of those who you want to talk to and those who you just talk to cuz they are with you. One of those people even if you are not open to all people you might still talk to her as if you were friends for the past decade.

Have you ever heard a melody? And the person behind you has to shake you to get you out of that imaginary world that succumbs you the moment you see someone.

That was my first sightseeing her. Let's call her "Lavanya". I was standing in front of the queue going for lunch on a Wednesday (we used to get potato veggies for lunch that day).

Lavanya and I met in class 5 all thanks to my mum sending me for French and not Sanskrit. Still thinking instead of "Bonjour," I would have been doing "Suprabaath" right now.

We met in the French class. I remember being late for the first class and the only empty seat was beside her. The thing is that then I believed love, at first sight, was true. And man, I was really in love with her. Now, I see, you know rays of light coming from behind the chair. The teacher brings me back from the dream, saying that I must help her by sitting down as she is supposed to teach and not me. So, as embarrassed as, I could be, I quietly went and sat down on the empty chair, Beside HER!! Turned out she was very friendly, she was the only one not laughing then (just giggles). But when I sat down there she said nothing, but just smiled and continued studying, for a moment, I thought she read my mind. We started talking for some reason which I can't recall. We became good friends and then on keeping a seat for each other during French and we used to bunk the class, not going out, but, we would talk during the class. I had this plan, that if we both don't study, then she will talk to me on the account of studying together. Never happened, although. Well, we were on the same level back then, but she was the shy one. I went ahead and aced in the French olympiad. Then one day all of a sudden I remember her becoming concerned, I remember that was the first time I saw that expression on her face. That was cuz my silly brother planned to do stunts near the pool and got his head stitched later at the infirmary. But it felt good that she was concerned for my brother, well, so was I and the rest of the people there, but, her concern was the thing that caught my eye. Well, the friend's ship bloomed, and she becomes my crush. Oh, I remember the Himachal trip we had in class 6 she came along, well, did I tell you about the rejection I faced earlier. Oh, you missed a good part. Well, what happens is that I have this silly douchebag friend of mine who tells me to "confess" my feeling to her cuz it might just be late by the time I do it. So I, like an idiot goes and like any other creep tell her "hey Lavanya, I love you" nothing else just that and I wait there like an idiot expecting her to reciprocate the same. but OFC she rejected saying "we're good friends together"...... Well, nothing wrong with that cuz looking back at it today, oh, I am so relieved we're still friends!! Well, I have done many silly things back then I still do a few of them the less intense ones now but why change for the world. "the people who come to live somewhere learn about the place, and the person who comes to rule the place teachers the place about him."

Well thoughts apart, we were never too much available for each other that we would have been over the other we still meet till date and you know we're good friends like we were back in the days.

She likes dancing I remember, she had this liking for classical (Indian classical) and she was pretty good at it. If I am not wrong played badminton the year she met the love of her life. Well, it all begins with me OFC!! I was a good friend of his and one day I took him to the badminton court after him nagging for the whole day just to the glimpse of my "crush". Well, he was like bro, she's love at first sight type. How can't anyone fall for her? I felt good but didn't realize he by anyone meant him. But with some help, he was, able to, you know propose to her and you know what she accepted. No hard feeling they look good together. And after all, I still have the best friend's post I wasn't removed from that.

Well, I had this so-called closure one-sided one in the nationals we went to. Well, didn't, I tell you we were on the kickboxing team together? Well, she was pretty good at it, I was a bronzer but when she came she went for the head of the trophy and brought gold.

Well, she was my first crush and I have had a hell of a roller coaster ride with her. That's our little secret do you remember, well to the readers don't bother thinking. (wink)

She taught me that in a relationship the two people might not have to be boyfriend/girlfriend but sometimes they are just friends, sometimes a shoulder to cry on, and sometimes even strangers. That's my relationship with her.

Then I found someone I found to be then 'my type'..........

CHAPTER THREE

First Relation...

It all started in class 7, and I was starting to accept it after Lavanya started dating. I was seated on a bench in the first row, near the classroom's entrance. Then this girl I remember made me go through all of my emotions all over again. But this time I didn't tell anyone and kept it in my heart's locker. Then she entered the same room. My teacher was standing behind her. Miss. Vandana, my class teacher, introduced her to the class as Palak. That name was all over my mind from then on. Was I ready for all this again?

But I wasn't sure until my friend hit me with his elbow as a gesture to shift as she wanted to sit beside me during school; I felt strange at first but was excited deep down; we talked all day that day. I wasn't the most studious person. I've always preferred self-study or watching videos on YouTube. However, from where I belong, home-schooling was not an option. So, when I was six years old, I was placed in a boarding school. But that's a different story. She was the same way.

I remember her friend pushing her to tie me a Rakhi (an Indian festival in which sisters tie a ribbon of protection around their brothers' wrists and the brother presents her with gifts and promises to protect her for a lifetime). She simply said, "I can't," and walked away. She was beside me that day. But she didn't say anything to me. She simply gave me a glance or a stare from time to time. It made me feel awkward, but also good. There's this thing about us boys. We will not tell you that we like or love you until we feel insecure; instead, we will begin talking to you on a regular basis. The staring and shyness became habitual after that. But she talked a lot to me, and oh! That infuriated her friend; I'm sorry, but I never wanted that. Time passed, and she realized Palak had feelings for me; I didn't, and neither did my so-called "Love Guru" friend.

Then there was the day when I was cornered in class, and her friend, who had already realized my feelings for Palak, handed me a paper to read. My buddy had sent a proposal letter to Palak. I was in a state of disarray because he had exposed me. So, keeping my cool, I said, "Let me explain." It's not what you think; I enjoy our friendship, but I've liked you since the day you arrived at this school, the day you entered this classroom, and introduced yourself". Her jaws were wide open as a result of this. The next thing she said was that she wanted me to commit suicide. She stated, "What happened? This isn't your friend's letter. And why didn't you tell me earlier, but if we date, you should stop using the lingo your friends use around here ". I couldn't believe what had just happened, so I asked her to pinch me. She did, indeed, pinch me. And it was painful. I went daydreaming for lunch, like any other lover boy, and ate nothing.

I couldn't believe that destiny would take such a turn that the girl liked me back in the span of not even a complete month.

In class 7, we had a coral recitation competition. We had the most fun during the entire session. For the rest of the day, we're just lost in those black eyes, holding hands.

I remember messing with her hair. the soft silky hair she wore in a single ponytail.

As time passed, I was contacted by the coordinator's office. It was nothing out of the ordinary for me because I was on the student council. When I arrived, I noticed Palak sitting in the chair in front of the coordinator. According to the coordinator, I was apparently distracting this young girl from her studies and harassing her by constantly nagging her. Ma'am thought it was important to hear the other side of the story because I was also a student at the school. I informed her that we were good friends. So I assumed because whenever I spoke to her, she always responded. Finally, I asked the coordinator to change the sections. Which was met with a resounding no. Given that it was mid-session. So we began sitting at the two ends of the classroom, and by two ends, I mean the diagonal ones.

CHAPTER FOUR

First Friend...

If you're reading this chapter I'll assume you've come all the way here and not jumped your way to this chapter.

This is about another special person in my life. It's happiness (Khushi). She was really the happiness in my sad, broken life. My crush friend-zoned me, and my girlfriend donno why gave me up.

We had this park where the new "Meghavee" stands. I met Khushi in that park, I was on the swing swinging away as usual. She came up to me and demanded I gave her the swing at once. I without saying anything just got up and left. This continued for some days. Then I started to hang around with my then friends now sisters. We used to play this stupid game called '21' in which one person could only count 3 no.'s in a chance and the person ending on the 21st no. had to choose between "truth", "dare"... Turned out she was in the group too, slowly the game became interesting as we started to know about each other. All thanks to the dares the girls gave. No one took them all went with "truth". And the both of us used to get caught most of the time. So, we knew a few things about each other. We then started to hang around and whatsoever happened our bond just became concrete. But do you know that concrete also had a weakness, feelings? Now, you see being with someone for so long, makes you love them. If you don't enjoy someone's company you won't hang around with them for so long. We became like a couple for the world, but we were always friends within.

She was always scared of horror and haunted stuff. Yet she came along when I wanted to check out the haunted house or watch a horror movie. We would go for all these in groups, but in the end, it was just the both of us. Just us enjoying each- other. The feeling, the vibe around her was different to what I felt around Lavanya or Palak. She of course was an individual with a differentiating factor and most probably I liked that factor.

Even today we are best of friends. Well, at least I am still tagged in her posts so. I'll assume that's true.

Hey Khushi,

I know you'll read this someday. So, maybe our journey was a short one together, but we had this quality time together. And that's what life's about you leave people behind to meet new people. There is this void left in the heart when someone leaves and there's always someone who comes to fill that void. If not completely, at least give it a short. You were that person to me. And never be sad about things all things are temporary. What is permanent is the bond that you make on the way. (my philosophy)

CHAPTER FIVE

Patch Up.....

Time passed and I graduated in class 8. Now the thing is that it was me, last year with a metaphorical rose in my hand going to propose to Palak, that too the unexpected one. This year we were both batch holders. I had run for the president's post, but lost, So I ended up as the 'discipline in-charge head', on the other hand, I remember her being the environment minister. I, as usual, was on duty on a fine Tuesday, when suddenly two figures which I never expected to ever approach me came straight to my face. And pulled me aside. With a flower in her hand, Palak proposed to me in the corridors where I was supposed to be doing my duty of maintaining the decorum of the students. I was awestruck by the proposal, but I still loved her. So, keeping my self-respect aside, I accepted her. I was very happy that day I forgot about my duty and left everyone to their selves and to my surprise they behaved themselves without my continuous presence. But that is not the point I was with her after that, this time was a bit different. This time she was all over me and I was all over her as usual.

We were in Love. Me, I guess for the very first time. Well, who knows the feeling for the first time. The problem with our meeting this time was that we were in 2 distantly different sections I was in section A and she was in D. So, our meeting was very difficult, yet we found a way. Till the school breaks, we would have this notebook that she brought. I remember it was a black and blue classmate's notebook. I was the one who usually used to reply in that notebook. Because she only took it home on the weekends. It was a mutual decision to keep her out of trouble.

That year we had this sports week it was a 6-day event, Monday- Saturday. We could be with our friends and enjoy all facilities available at the school premises during school hours. OFC, I was glued to her section for the week. I did not sit with her, instead the first 3 days I was sitting behind her. Her turning around to talk to me made me feel special. Then on the 4th day, she started to sit with me. Even when she was sitting in front we used to hold hands for likely the whole day. We forgot about everyone and everything when we were together, I remember during the vocals she sang "I love you" a song from the movie "Bodyguard" for me. All of us were singing, but we were looking at each other and singing without a single glance at the lyrics. It was a really beautiful moment.

Then came teacher's day. The boarders had revisions in the mornings. So we had come for the same, She snuck me out of the room to her and we were there again sitting with her hands in mine. And me playing with her hair, the silence in the room was so intense, even when my friends were howling and shouting on top of their voices. The silence was not physical it was emotional. Our hearts were beating together. At the same pace and the same beat.

I remember her not liking arts and crafts, but yet coming for helping the teachers there, everyone except the teachers there knew the reason she was there, (That still makes me feel wicked). And I had this idiot friend who spilled color on her white shirt and spoiled it. She took it as a joke and asked me for my shirt. That was what I loved about her, She let things and people go easily. I never knew what I loved about her would backstab me.

I have always loved traveling. And that's why I went for 2 trips in 8th standard. 3 actually, but the 3rd was a family one. 2 out of the 3 were international. I went to Indonesia and U.S.A. Indonesia for my birthday and the U.S.A. For a school excursion. I might have gone there alone, but we were in touch for the almost the whole trip. Communication during the returning was a little problematic due to me being a Nepalese and traveling from India. But when I join my classes,

I find out that, my love, my girlfriend is dating one of the students. It was a shock for me, I wasn't sure if We were really over so I just asked her what the scenario was? She ignored me as if I was a complete strangers to each other. Me acting as dumb as I could, went straight to the boy and told him to stay away from her cuz she was mine...

Few-weeks passed, I left meeting people, I started being alone, depressed. She on the other hand moved on with no hesitation. Then all the emotions that I had prisoned in a box deep inside broke out, crashing the sky on me. He said something really not apt about her. The moment I found out. It was during lunch on a Wednesday, I just left the plate on the table and went straight to his class. Without any thoughts just gave him a good beating. The point is not that I acted Heroically, But the fact is I was also beaten by the guy and my life's first undertaking was signed. And yes, she didn't give a fuck to what I had done.

If you're reading this you're one of the best friends I might have made in my middle school. And Yes, I emphasize on the word Friend because I was just not ready for the throw back you gave me.

CHAPTER SIX

Dear Crush....

How can I convey my love to you when I have no obstacles to experiencing your affection? How can I write about my love for you when I have no words to express my feelings for you? You taught me how to love you with all of my heart and how to purify your love with all of my soul. My love for you is simple and profound, with feelings and pleasure pouring towards you every day.

You're exceptional, and I'll never forget you; if there's anyone I regard to be closest to my heart, it's you. I may have a lot of friends in my life, but none of them will be as important to me as you are; you're the one person I'll never be able to replace; we may not speak for days, months, or even years, but our relationship will always be there. I won't be unhappy with you if you don't text or respond to my texts frequently; it's alright since you were there for me when I needed you the most and have always been the reason for that smile on my face. You have always shared my anguish, and if I am sad, you are the one who notices it first, no one else. I've met many people in my life, but I doubt I'll ever meet anyone like you. Cos you're unique. I'll never forget you because you're not just a person, but a part of my heart that lived in this human body, reminding me of how much I'll always remember, care for, and love you no matter what. I will forget to tell you many things, but I want you to know how much you mean to me and how memorable you are in my life.

I may not be a permanent part of your life, but I am perfectly content to be a temporary part of it. But I want to be the finest temporary person you've ever had.

When anything truly fantastic happens, I miss you because you're the one person I'll ever want to share it with. I miss you when anything bothers me because you are the one person who truly knows me. I miss you when I laugh and cry because I know you're the one who helps my laughter increase and my tears fade. I miss you all the time, but especially while I'm awake in my bed at night. And remember the lovely moments we had together; those were the best and most unforgettable experiences of my life.

You're mine and I'm not ever letting you go, because you're my special and fave person, don't ever tell me that "You're too good for me" or "I deserve someone better" because no one can make me happy as you do, I won't lie to you, I won't ever make you miserable I promise, I know, I argue with you, I may have acted worse, but I can never stop caring or loving you because you matter to me a lot from the day we met, but none are as essential as you, none have dried my tears, or made me smile vocally, you have, and you have heard my experiences as well. You've made me laugh, if I ever make you sad, I apologize. I'll try not to ever make you angry, I'll irritate you cuz that's my birthright, but, I swear, I'll never make you weep because you're that precious to me.

I love you now, not tomorrow, not someday, but right now. I believe in you, I admire you, and I want you. And you can be wrong a lot of the time, and we can fight and get ridiculously angry at each other, but nothing in this world can change the fact that I love you.

I'm going to love you in your weakest moments to your strongest ones. I'm going to still love you the most, when you're sad. I'll always be here I ain't going anywhere. I want to hug you, I want you with all your imperfections and skills. And I'm always going to want you, I'm always going yo be there with you even if you leave yourself.

CHAPTER SEVEN

Finally Love...

I didn't actually meet her until a year and a half later. She had been in Section C since eighth grade. If you're wondering why all of his stories begin or end in eighth grade, let me explain. So here's the deal: the covid-19 pandemic broke out after 8th grade. This was the most difficult time for the world, The economy was in shambles, and many people's lives were on the verge of being extinguished. The sad part of it all is that it took a pandemic for us to realize, that we can be helpful to our fellow humans.

Coming back to the point, I saw her during the online classes, and this time I didn't get lost or something. I just wanted to see her very often then-on. Not realizing it had become a regular thing. And I was basically stalking her. I really liked her and wanted to talk to her. Well, I got the chance during the 1st term of the class 10 board examination. I couldn't do it, I just walked away. Cuz I didn't know what I would say when I actually met her.

Then things began to normalize and we came back to school. And I met her again, this time during the pre-board exams. And guess what I met her with the unexpected help of "21" Remember that game? We began talking and my friends started to notice what I felt. I have always been really bad at hiding my feelings for people.

We began talking thereafter. The best part was she had a crush. So, it was a never-ending pursuit for me. And guess what I already knew that she had many 'crushers' around. We started to talk, but then we were on Snapchat which I got that very day. The talking was less as it was awkward for both of us to talk to someone both in-person and via text.

Holi (A festival of colors, where you come together with your friends and enjoy playing with colors and eating sweets, It basically marks the return of colors in one's black and white life). And, this Holi actually did. It brought you as color in my life. I might have never even talked to you properly before that day, But yet in silence we were together for the whole time that day. In one way or the other. You were the first person to play with me that day. If you didn't notice. Each and every moment of that day is still fresh in my memories.

Even after Holi was over it kept helping us talk. Actually, it is what brought your phone no. For me. You wanted the pics. And, I couldn't give it via Snapchat. Then our chats actually started. It wasn't much as usual, but now we weren't awkward. I still remember you texting me on both the apps and me trying to cope up with your pace.

I also proposed to you on the 23rd of March, it was less of a proposal and more of a question from your end. You asked me and even if I wanted to stop myself. My heart just typed your name that day.

Time flew and we went home, we had Snapchat but, being with you in person had its feel to it. We had our boards nearing. So we focused on studies. I literally can't believe this, but I waited the whole day for someone to wish me. It didn't matter if the rest of the world did or not. When you wished me, I actually felt that it was my birthday, that day. I was so happy that day. I then understood that on birthdays you might get 50 messages, 20 calls, maybe if you're that famous 15 tags, and countless notifications. But the very next day, Great Silence.

Then came your birthday. I wanted to say so many things, but I couldn't. So. here it is:

Happy birthday to my favorite person in the entire world. I'm not sure where to begin, but I have a lot to say to you. Today, I just want to say "Thank you for being in my life," thanks for being the person on whom I can always rely. You're the sweetest, cutest, and most wonderful person I've ever met. It's your birthday, and I can't keep calm; I'm getting excited. I've always looked forward to this day because I wanted to make you feel special, to show you that "you're so important to me," and to "upload your photos," which I had safely stored. I love you and will always love you; you are the best thing that has ever happened to me. You're so caring and down to earth that I know I'll never find anyone like you, and even if I do, I know they won't be able to tolerate me as well as you do because you know me from the inside out, you make me laugh, you make me angry, but at the end of the day, I can't survive being angry at you. I don't know how I'll get through a day without you, and by the way, you're adorable when you're angry. I'm possessive of you because you're my special person and I don't want to share you with anyone; this birthday, I want to wish you a very happy birthday; don't expect a gift because the best gift you have is...

We finally met after the study leave. It was the "Blessings Ceremony" where we met because you betrayed us and stayed back at home to prepare for your exams. But the little time that I had with you after you know all the chasing by few people we got a little privacy and all I did was just stare in those eyes.

Then meeting you every day during the exams at the examination center. Those 5 mins before and after the exams were enough for you to understand everything on my mind. Then came the dark era when your Snapchat was caught. We then only had those 5 mins to talk. Slowly that too was taken away.

Well, my love, there is no end to the love in my heart for you, but you have seen our future as friends, so be it. People always don't need to say "I love you" sometimes it could also sound like: "Be safe", "Did you eat?" or "Call me when you reach home".

We met as strangers
We became friends
From friends, We became Besties who can't live
without the other,
Now again, we're strangers.

But remember even if we get separated, whenever you're low just giving me a call you'll always find me outside with a bouquet of roses, a pack of Tissues and your favorite sin.

I want you to remember something. Know that no matter what comes our way, I will never stop loving you. You give me feelings that nobody has ever given me.

Feelings of the purest, most genuine happiness that anyone could ever have. I don't care how corny, I sound, Our souls were made for each other and you know it. We're supposed to be together. Everything about us being together makes sense. We are my definition of perfect. You have the ability to make everything okay even when it's not. You're my home. I could be anywhere in the world, but as long as I am with you I know I'll be okay. I know I'll be safe. I know I'll be happy. I love you in ways I never knew were possible and I hope that never changes. I want to thank you to make me the luckiest man in the entire world, maybe I won't get what I expect but, what we have in between us. This friendship is the sweetest reason to die gladly for.

If you think that's the end you're mistaken life goes on and so will my journals.

but until the next meeting

Adios Amigos!!

9 798887 331591

Printed by Libri Plureos GmbH in Hamburg, Germany